# A Blue Kind of Day

by Rachel Tomlinson

illustrated by
**Tori-Jay Mordey**

Kokila

Coen was having a blue kind of day. . . .
It was a slumping, sighing, sobbing kind of day.

Gloomy feelings filled up Coen's entire body, and he was sure that everybody could see blue radiating from his skin.

The feelings were such a deep,
murky kind of blue that they made
Coen feel trapped.

His body felt prickly, tense,

and wound up like a coil.

He dragged himself back to bed
and scrunched into a tight, angry ball.
Coen was never going to get out of bed ever again.

Mum sat down gently next to Coen. "Just pull the covers back and get out of bed. It can't be that bad." She patted Coen's shoulder.

Coen snuggled deeper into his blankets. Feeling blue made his body so heavy that he just couldn't get out of bed.

Dad peered into Coen's bedroom and smiled. "Let's go outside and toss the football around! I always feel better when I get some fresh air."

But Coen didn't want anyone to see his muddled-up, blue feelings. So he pulled the blankets tight around himself like armor.

His little sister, Junie, pounced on him.

"You don't look sick!

What's wrong with you?"

she demanded.

Coen felt like a lost kite: loose in the breeze, with feelings that tangled like string. He couldn't find the words to describe why everything felt so wrong, so instead he tucked safely into himself like a turtle.

Mum told her funniest joke;

dad pulled a silly face;

and Junie grabbed Coen's favorite teddy to show him.

Coen rolled away from them to face the wall. He just did not feel like laughing or smiling today. His family looked at one another with concern, but they weren't ready to give up just yet.

One by one, they snuggled closer to Coen and waited.

They waited because feelings cannot be rushed.

They waited because it was okay that Coen felt blue.

They waited because they knew that Coen's
blue feelings would not last forever.

They waited until Coen was ready.

Coen lay still for a very long time. He noticed how warm it felt to snuggle with his family.

MYTHS AND LEGENDS OF TORRES STRAIT

As the warmth spread through his body, Coen found that his blue feelings weren't quite so deep and murky anymore.

"Can you tell me a story?" Coen whispered.

As his mother read, her soft, calm voice settled over him, and Coen felt his body uncoiling and unclenching.

His tiptoeing fingers crept out from under the blanket to grasp his dad's hand, and the confused feelings started to untangle.

Peep.

Rustle.

Tumble.

Coen slowly emerged from his blanket cocoon and smiled at his family.

And then he wondered what tomorrow might bring.

# Author's Note

Children learn about feelings in the same way they practice their ABCs and 123s, with guidance from their caregiver(s)! Emotions are not good or bad, they are simply messages that tell us something important. It is normal to feel sad and down sometimes. Things don't always go our way; we get disappointed; we experience loss and other adverse life events. But depression is more than sadness.

It can impact thought patterns and reactions to the world and also result in physical symptoms. Depression can be challenging to identify in children because they might lack the language to tell us. All they can really understand and express is how it makes their bodies feel. Here are examples of depressive symptoms to look out for in your child:

- Challenges concentrating/paying attention
- Change in appetite (less or excessively hungry)
- Trouble sleeping (falling asleep, staying asleep, or sleeping too much)
- Somatic (physical) changes (muscle tension; feeling exhausted, heavy, or weighed down; slumping; stomachaches; headaches; etc.)
- Expressing big emotions (irritation, frustration, sadness, distress, worry, etc.)
- Avoidance of things they usually enjoy, including social situations

**How to support your child if they are experiencing symptoms of depression or emotional distress:**

It's normal to want to "fix" or resolve an issue in order to make your child feel better, but we can accidentally invalidate our children's experience by rushing to action.

Some emotions (like anger) result in excess energy, so an option could be to do jumping jacks, skip, or squeeze dough to help cope. Other emotions (like sadness and fear) zap our energy, so young people might want to rest quietly or engage their senses with positive things (like cuddling a favorite teddy or listening to a favorite song).

Read books to your children where they can see themselves reflected, and get them thinking about the main characters' emotions: "How do you think they feel? Why?" You can then prompt with insights like "Can you see their face? They have tears; what might that tell us?"

Draw an outline of a person, and give your child different colored pens. Get them to match a color to a feeling and encourage them to color in different areas of the body where they feel different emotions.

If behaviors or thoughts persist for more than two weeks or there is a marked change from your child's usual behaviors or thoughts, it is important to seek professional support and advice.

—Rachel Tomlinson,
registered psychologist

*I live and work on Whadjuk land, and acknowledge the people of the First Nation and traditional custodians of the land. I pay my respect to them, their culture and to elders past, present and emerging. To all the children finding their way through big feelings: I see you. You've got this!*
**–R. T.**


*To my family, my nephew, and my goddaughter.*
**–T. J. M.**


Kokila acknowledges with deep respect the resilience and resistance of First Nations people across Australia, their Elders past and present, and their many unsung heroes who work tirelessly to overcome the impacts of colonization and maintain their ancient, vibrant cultures. A donation to the Magabala Books Fund will coincide with the publication of this book.

Kokila
An imprint of Penguin Random House LLC, New York

First published in the United States of America by Kokila, an imprint of Penguin Random House LLC, 2022

Text copyright © 2022 by Rachel Tomlinson
Illustrations copyright © 2022 by Tori-Jay Mordey

Visit us online at penguinrandomhouse.com.

Library of Congress Cataloging-in-Publication Data is available.

Manufactured in China
ISBN 9780593324011

1 3 5 7 9 10 8 6 4 2
HH

Design by Jasmin Rubero
Text set in Clavo Book

*The artist created the illustrations digitally and loosely based the character design on her own family.*